BEARS

Story by **RUTH KRAUSS**

Pictures by **PHYLLIS ROWAND**

SCHOLASTIC INC.

New York Toronto London Auckland Sydney

ISBN 0-590-01546-X

24 23 22 21 20 19 18 17 16 15 14   8 9/8 0/9

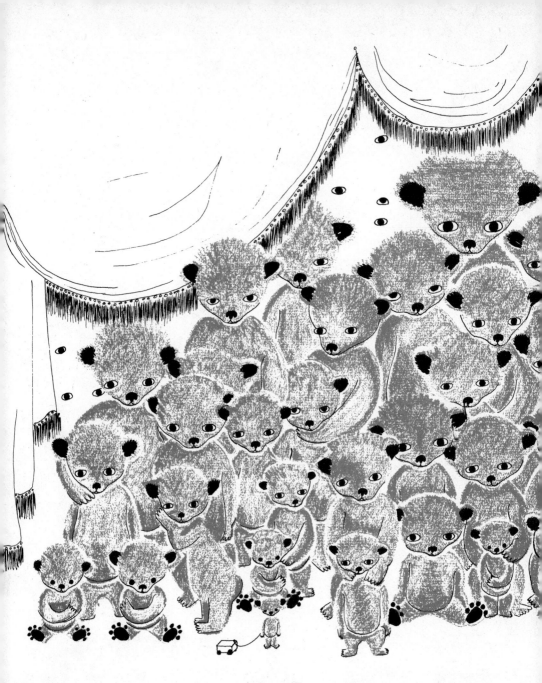

Bears, bears, bears,

bears, bears.

On the stairs

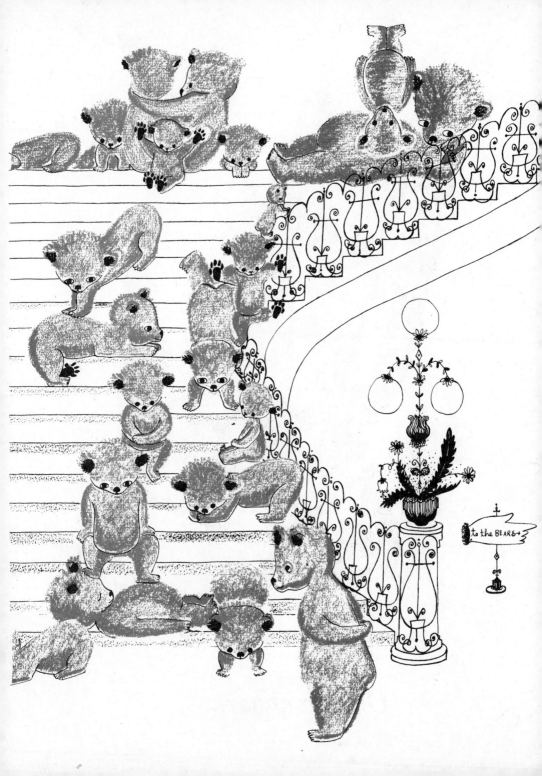

to the BEARS

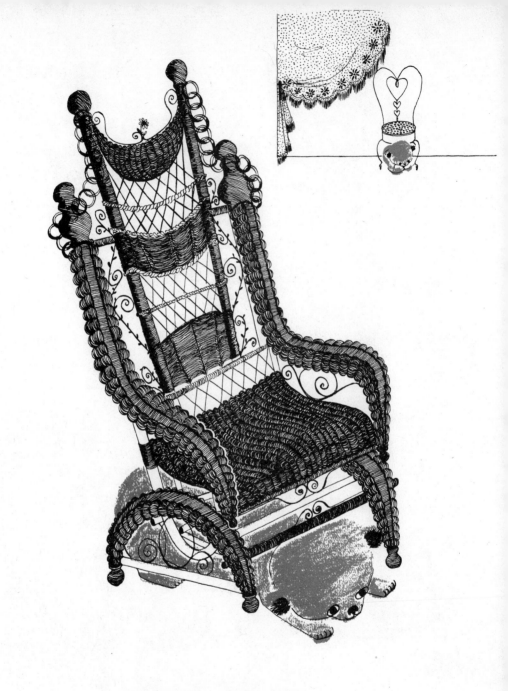

Under chairs

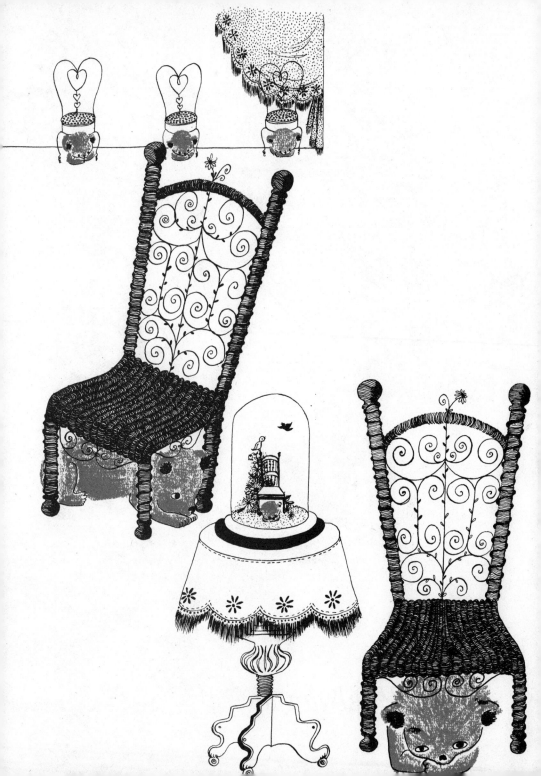

Washing hairs

Giving stares

Collecting fares

Stepping in squares

Millionaires

Everywheres

Bears, bears, bears, bears, bears.